This book belongs to:

_____

_____

Story by
Pina Mastromonaco

Illustrations by
David Martin

MERRY LANE PRESS

To Jeffrey and Victoria,
the best storytellers I know.

—Pina

For Patti,
with all my love.

—David

Merry Lane Press, a children's book publisher,
educates, entertains, and expands children's understanding
of the world in which they live.

Merry Lane Press also encourages our family of talented
individuals to explore new horizons and embrace new ideas.

Library of Congress Control Number: 2004116180
ISBN 0-9744307-1-4

Printed in China

For more information about our books, and the authors and artists
who create them, e-mail us at: alan@merrylanepress.com, or
visit our website: www.merrylanepress.com.

Merry Lane Press, 18 E. 16th Street, New York, NY 10003

King Bartholomew was a selfish king who played a lot and ruled very little. He loved riddles, puzzles, and word games. He loved chess, checkers, and dominoes. Of course, it was no surprise that his toy collection was the biggest in the land.

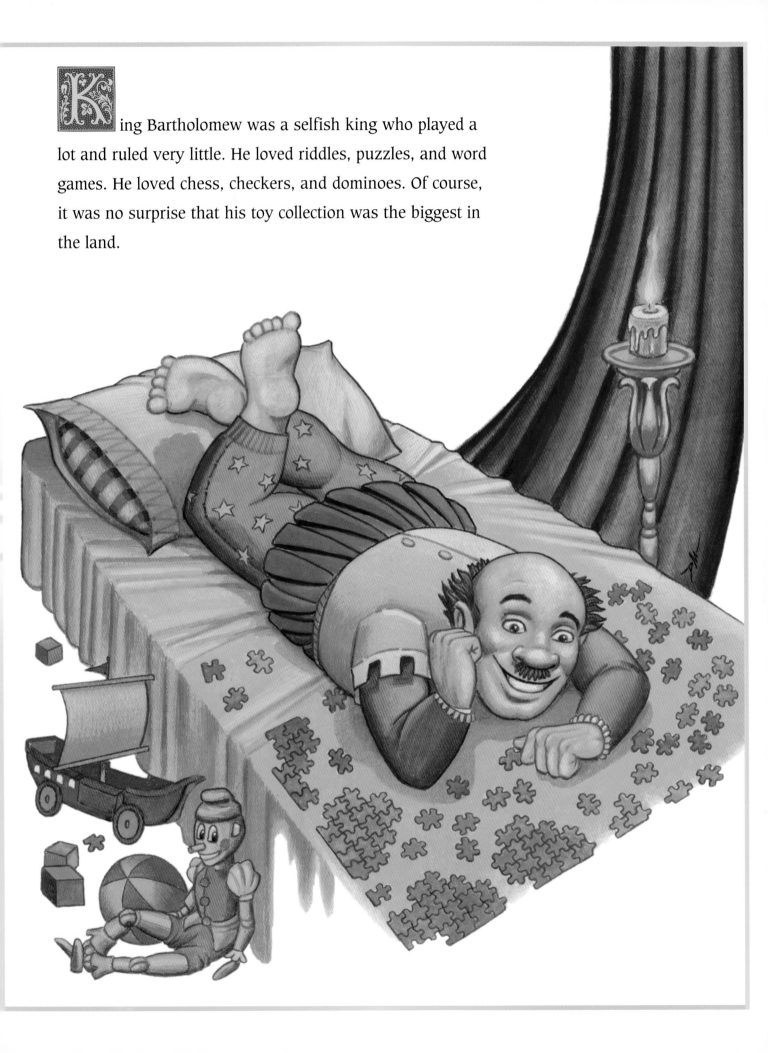

His most trusted friend, the court jester, provided King Bartholomew with all the riddles, puzzles, and word games his heart desired.

"What goes up and down without moving?" The court jester read from her scroll.

"Why stairs, of course," replied the king.

"What's full of holes but still holds water?"

"That's easy, too: a sponge," replied the king.

"What turns everything around, but does not move?"

The king thought hard. Then he smiled and said, "A mirror. There is no riddle I cannot solve," he declared.

Just then, two royal servants appeared carrying a great big puzzle.

When the king finished piecing it together, he thought he was looking in a mirror.

"You must hang this up at once so I can admire it every day," said the king to his servants.

But they were not sure they could do that. "Where will we find the nail and hammer?"

King Bartholomew was puzzled.

"It's hard to find anything in this kingdom—except dice in the goblets, puzzle pieces in the stables, and chess pieces in the ballroom," said one servant.

"What is he talking about?" the king asked the court jester.

The court jester opened the door to the garden and said, "Perhaps the kingdom would be in better order if you spent less time playing and more time ruling."

"The kingdom is in perfect order," replied the king.

"That's not true," said the court jester. "The crops need planting, the mill needs cleaning, and the town bridge needs repairs. If you don't look into these things, who will?"

King Bartholomew would not hear any of it. "I am king so I can do whatever I want. Now please give me a new riddle. One that will challenge my royal intelligence and keep my mind off of my royal duties."

The court jester bowed politely before the king and sang out, "If it's a difficult riddle you want, then it's a difficult riddle you shall receive."

The court jester tried to come up with the perfect riddle. She knew the king would like a riddle that was about him. This gave her a great idea. She wrote frantically on her scroll.

This riddle sounds difficult, but is so simple. The king will be pleased, thought the court jester. When she was done, she blew out her candle and went to sleep.

The next morning, the king summoned the court jester to the palace.

"You had an entire night to think up a challenging riddle," he said. "I hope you used your time wisely."

"Indeed I have, Your Majesty," replied the court jester. She danced around in delight. "This is my most clever riddle yet."

She took out her scroll, cleared her throat, and sang out, "What belongs only to you, King Bartholomew, but is used most often by those around you?"

"What do you mean?" King Bartholomew could not believe his ears.

"I knew you would like it, King Bartholomew," said the court jester.

Before she could bow in triumph, the king roared. "Is it my puzzles? My games? My tops? My Jack-in-the-box? What can it be?" The king gasped. "Is it my scepter? My crown? My horse? My cape?"

"It's none of those things," she replied. "Take some time to think about it, when you solve it, you will see how clever a riddle it is."

"I have no time to think," he said. "I must speak to my subjects immediately and get back what's mine. What's mine is only mine, and no one else can use it."

The townspeople gathered around the palace grounds to listen to King Bartholomew speak.

"It has come to my attention that you, the people I thought I could trust, are betraying me," declared the king.

"What is he talking about?" said one man in the crowd.

"He must be losing his mind," said another.

"I have been told that you have been using something that belongs to me. **I want it back this instant**!" he yelled.

No one came forward.

"Very well then, you are all banished from the palace grounds. From this day forward you no longer have a king," said King Bartholomew.

The court jester tried to stop the madness by telling King Bartholomew the answer, but the furious king would not listen. He pointed to the door and asked even the court jester to leave.

The king shut the gate and locked the doors. "No one can touch my precious possessions now."

He sat on his throne and looked around. He saw his games, puzzles, and toys and knew just what he would do. And so day after day, dawn until dusk, the king played to his heart's content. He did not miss his people. He did not think of the court jester. He just played and played and played.

After a few weeks, the king had pieced together all his puzzles, finished all the crosswords, and figured out all the word games. His Jack-in-the-box did not make him laugh anymore, and his tops were not as interesting as they used to be. He looked around for something new.

"Chess!" he yelled. He ran to the chess set, dusted off the pieces, and made his first move. Playing alone was not going to work.

"Checkers!" he yelled. He ran to the checkerboard, dusted off the pieces, and made his first move. That was not going to work, either.

Slouched on his throne, the king heard a bird chirping outside the palace window. He went to get a closer look, but the startled bird flew away.

I'll feel better tomorrow, thought the king.

But the next day, nothing changed. Instead of playing, the king paced up and down his garden. From a distance, he watched the townspeople. For the first time since the banishment, the king felt lonely. He wished he could be with his people.

The king opened his doors and waited. But no one came.

That evening, the court jester was surprised to find the king knocking on her door.

"I've opened my doors, but no one has come to see me," said the king.

"Are you sure you want them back?" she asked. "Since you have banished everyone from the palace, no one in the land has used that which is yours."

"I'm glad to hear that," he said.

The court jester bowed politely and said, "Your Majesty, if others could use that which is yours then you would not be so lonely."

"I am not lonely," the king lied. "I have my games to keep me company."

"Then you will not be interested in coming to the carnival tonight?" asked the court jester.

The king did not answer.

That night, the king sat by the palace window and listened to the jolly hoots and hollers of the townspeople at the carnival.

For the first time, the king did not care if others used his possessions. The only thing he wanted was to be with his people. He pushed his games and toys aside and went to join them.

As the king neared the carnival he had a thought. *What if they don't want to be with me? What if they have forgotten about their king?*

But when the people saw the king they welcomed him with warm greetings.

The king was so happy to be with his townspeople again that he made a promise to them, "I am sorry. I have been so selfish. You are welcome to use everything that belongs to me," he declared. "From this day forward, I promise to take better care of the kingdom and better care of you."

"Thank you, King Bartholomew," said one man.

"That is very generous, King Bartholomew," said a woman curtsying.

"I'm glad you changed your mind, King Bartholomew," added the court jester.

King Bartholomew liked the sound of his name used by his townspeople.

"That's it!" he sang out, "The riddle, I understand the riddle! What belongs only to me, but is used most often by those around me, is my **name**, King Bartholomew!"

From then on, King Bartholomew ruled just enough, and played only after he had tended to his kingdom and his loyal subjects.